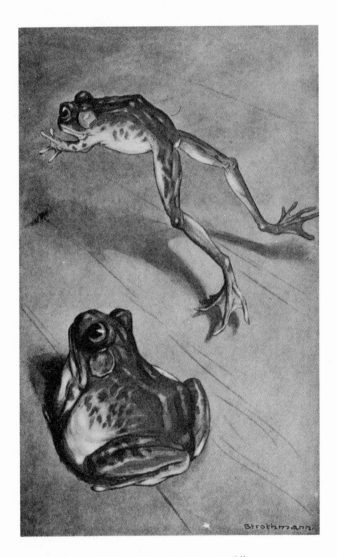

"'ONE—TWO—THREE—*GIT!*'"

The Jumping Frog

IN ENGLISH, THEN IN FRENCH, THEN
CLAWED BACK INTO A CIVILIZED
LANGUAGE ONCE MORE BY
PATIENT, UNREMUNERATED TOIL

By Mark Twain

ILLUSTRATED BY
F. STROTHMANN

DOVER PUBLICATIONS, INC.
NEW YORK

Published in Canada by General Publishing Company, Ltd., 30 Lesmill Road, Don Mills, Toronto, Ontario.

Published in the United Kingdom by Constable and Company, Ltd., 10 Orange Street, London WC 2.

This Dover edition, first published in 1971, is an unabridged and unaltered republication of the work originally published by Harper & Brothers in 1903.

International Standard Book Number: 0-486-22686-7
Library of Congress Catalog Card Number: 79-142286

Manufactured in the United States of America
Dover Publications, Inc.
180 Varick Street
New York, N.Y. 10014

Illustrations

"'ONE—TWO—THREE—*GIT!*'" . *Frontispiece*

"I FOUND SIMON WHEELER DOZ-
ING COMFORTABLY" . . . *Facing p.* 4

"BACKED ME INTO A CORNER" . " 8

"'THISH-YER SMILEY HAD A
MARE'". . . . . . . " 12

"ANDREW JACKSON". . . . . " 18

"TURN ONE SUMMERSET, OR MAY-
BE A COUPLE'". . . . . " 24

"DAN'L WEBSTER" . . . . . " 30

"'IT MIGHT BE A CANARY, MAY-
BE, BUT IT AIN'T—IT'S ONLY
JUST A FROG'". . . . . " 36

"'PRIZED HIS MOUTH OPEN'" . " 42

"'FINALLY HE KETCHED A FROG'" " 48

"'TURNED HIM UPSIDE DOWN'" " 52

"MY RE-TRANSLATION FROM THE
FRENCH". . . . . . . " 56

The Jumping Frog

❧

E VEN a criminal is entitled to fair play; and certainly when a man who has done no harm has been unjustly treated, he is privileged to do his best to right himself. My attention has just been called to an article some three years old in a French magazine entitled, "Revue des Deux Mondes" (Review of Some Two Worlds), wherein the writer treats of "Les Humoristes Américaines" (These Humorists Americans). I am one of

The Jumping Frog

these humorists Americans dissected by him, and hence the complaint I am making.

This gentleman's article is an able one (as articles go, in the French, where they always tangle up everything to that degree that when you start into a sentence you never know whether you are going to come out alive or not). It is a very good article, and the writer says all manner of kind and complimentary things about me—for which I am sure I thank him with all my heart; but then why should he go and spoil all his praise by one unlucky experiment? What I refer to is this: he says my Jumping Frog is a funny story, but still he can't see why it should ever really convulse any one

The Jumping Frog

with laughter—and straightway pro-
ceeds to translate it into French in
order to prove to his nation that
there is nothing so very extrava-
gantly funny about it. Just there is
where my complaint originates. He
has not translated it at all; he has
simply mixed it all up; it is no more
like the Jumping Frog when he gets
through with it than I am like a
meridian of longitude. But my mere
assertion is not proof; wherefore I
print the French version, that all
may see that I do not speak falsely;
furthermore, in order that even the
unlettered may know my injury and
give me their compassion, I have been
at infinite pains and trouble to re-
translate this French version back
into English; and to tell the truth I

The Jumping Frog

have wellnigh worn myself out at it, having scarcely rested from my work during five days and nights. I cannot speak the French language, but I can translate very well, though not fast, I being self-educated. I ask the reader to run his eye over the original English version of the Jumping Frog, and then read the French or my retranslation, and kindly take notice how the Frenchman has riddled the grammar. I think it is the worst I ever saw, and yet the French are called a polished nation. If I had a boy that put sentences together as they do, I would polish him to some purpose. Without further introduction, the Jumping Frog, as I originally wrote it, was as follows [after it will be found the French version, and after the

4

"I FOUND SIMON WHEELER DOZING COMFORTABLY"

The Jumping Frog

latter my re - translation from the French]:

THE NOTORIOUS JUMPING FROG OF CALAVERAS* COUNTY

In compliance with the request of a friend of mine, who wrote me from the East, I called on good-natured, garrulous old Simon Wheeler, and inquired after my friend's friend, Leonidas W. Smiley, as requested to do, and I hereunto append the result. I have a lurking suspicion that *Leonidas W.* Smiley is a myth; that my friend never knew such a personage; and that he only conjectured that if I asked old Wheeler about him, it would remind him of his infamous *Jim* Smiley, and he would go to work

* Pronounced Cal-e-*va*-ras.

5

The Jumping Frog

and bore me to death with some exasperating reminiscence of him as long and as tedious as it should be useless to me. If that was the design, it succeeded.

I found Simon Wheeler dozing comfortably by the barroom stove of the dilapidated tavern in the decaying mining camp of Angel's, and I noticed that he was fat and bald-headed, and had an expression of winning gentleness and simplicity upon his tranquil countenance. He roused up, and gave me good-day. I told him a friend of mine had commissioned me to make some inquiries about a cherished companion of his boyhood named *Leonidas W.* Smiley — *Rev. Leonidas W.* Smiley, a young minister of the Gospel, who he had heard

The Jumping Frog

was at one time a resident of Angel's Camp. I added that if Mr. Wheeler could tell me anything about this Rev. Leonidas W. Smiley, I would feel under many obligations to him.

Simon Wheeler backed me into a corner and blockaded me there with his chair, and then sat down and reeled off the monotonous narrative which follows this paragraph. He never smiled, he never frowned, he never changed his voice from the gentle-flowing key to which he tuned his initial sentence, he never betrayed the slightest suspicion of enthusiasm; but all through the interminable narrative there ran a vein of impressive earnestness and sincerity, which showed me plainly that, so far from his imagining that there was any-

The Jumping Frog

thing ridiculous or funny about his
story, he regarded it as a really im-
portant matter, and admired its two
heroes as men of transcendent genius
in *finesse*. I let him go on in his own
way, and never interrupted him once.

"Rev. Leonidas W. H'm, Rever-
end Le—well, there was a feller here
once by the name of *Jim* Smiley, in
the winter of '49 — or maybe it was
the spring of '50—I don't recollect
exactly, somehow, though what
makes me think it was one or the
other is because I remember the big
flume warn't finished when he first
come to the camp; but anyway, he
was the curiosest man about always
betting on anything that turned up
you ever see, if he could get anybody
to bet on the other side; and if he

"BACKED ME INTO A CORNER"

The Jumping Frog

couldn't he'd change sides. Any way
that suited the other man would suit
him—any way just so's he got a bet,
he was satisfied. But still he was
lucky, uncommon lucky; he most always come out winner. He was always ready and laying for a chance;
there couldn't be no solit'ry thing
mentioned but that feller'd offer to
bet on it, and take ary side you
please, as I was just telling you. If
there was a horse-race, you'd find
him flush or you'd find him busted
at the end of it; if there was a dog-
fight, he'd bet on it; if there was a
cat-fight, he'd bet on it; if there was
a chicken-fight, he'd bet on it; why, if
there was two birds setting on a fence,
he would bet you which one would
fly first; or if there was a camp-meet-

The Jumping Frog

ing, he would be there reg'lar to bet on Parson Walker, which he judged to be the best exhorter about here, and so he was, too, and a good man. If he even see a straddle-bug start to go anywheres, he would bet you how long it would take him to get to—to wherever he was going to, and if you took him up, he would foller that straddle-bug to Mexico but what he would find out where he was bound for and how long he was on the road. Lots of the boys here has seen that Smiley, and can tell you about him. Why, it never made no difference to *him* — he'd bet an *any* thing — the dangdest feller. Parson Walker's wife laid very sick once, for a good while, and it seemed as if they warn't going to save her; but one morning

The Jumping Frog

he come in, and Smiley up and asked him how she was, and he said she was considable better — thank the Lord for his inf'nite mercy — and coming on so smart that with the blessing of Prov'dence she'd get well yet; and Smiley, before he thought, says: 'Well, I'll resk two-and-a-half she don't anyway.'

"Thish-yer Smiley had a mare— the boys called her the fifteen-minute nag, but that was only in fun, you know, because, of course, she was faster than that—and he used to win money on that horse, for all she was so slow and always had the asthma, or the distemper, or the consumption, or something of that kind. They used to give her two or three hundred yards start, and then pass her

The Jumping Frog

under way; but always at the fag
end of the race she'd get excited and
desperate like, and come cavorting
and straddling up, and scattering
her legs around limber, sometimes in
the air, and sometimes out to one
side among the fences, and kicking
up m-o-r-e dust and raising m-o-r-e
racket with her coughing and sneez-
ing and blowing her nose—and *always* fetch up at the stand just
about a neck ahead, as near as you
could cipher it down.

"And he had a little small bull-pup,
that to look at him you'd think he
warn't worth a cent but to set around
and look ornery and lay for a chance
to steal something. But as soon as
money was up on him he was a dif-
ferent dog; his under-jaw'd begin to

"'THISH-YER SMILEY HAD A MARE'"

The Jumping Frog

stick out like the fo'castle of a steam-
boat, and his teeth would uncover
and shine like the furnaces.   And a
dog might tackle him and bully-rag
him, and bite him, and throw him
over his shoulder two or three times,
and Andrew Jackson—which was the
name of the pup—Andrew Jackson
would never let on but what *he* was
satisfied, and hadn't expected nothing else—and the bets being doubled
and doubled on the other side all the
time, till the money was all up; and
then all of a sudden he would grab
that other dog jest by the j'int of
his hind leg and freeze to it—not
chaw, you understand, but only just
grip and hang on till they throwed
up the sponge, if it was a year.
Smiley always come out winner on

that pup, till he harnessed a dog once
that didn't have no hind legs, because they'd been sawed off in a cir-
cular saw, and when the thing had
gone along far enough, and the money
was all up, and he come to make a
snatch for his pet holt, he see in a
minute how he'd been imposed on,
and how the other dog had him in the
door, so to speak, and he 'peared surprised, and then he looked sorter
discouraged-like and didn't try no
more to win the fight, and so he got
shucked out bad. He give Smiley a
look, as much as to say his heart was
broke, and it was *his* fault, for putting
up a dog that hadn't no hind legs for
him to take holt of, which was his
main dependence in a fight, and then
he limped off a piece and laid down

14

The Jumping Frog

and died. It was a good pup, was that Andrew Jackson, and would have made a name for hisself if he'd lived, for the stuff was in him and he had genius—I know it, because he hadn't no opportunities to speak of, and it don't stand to reason that a dog could make such a fight as he could under them circumstances if he hadn't no talent. It always makes me feel sorry when I think of that last fight of his'n, and the way it turned out.

"Well, thish-yer Smiley had rat-tarriers, and chicken cocks, and tom-cats and all them kind of things, till you couldn't rest, and you couldn't fetch nothing for him to bet on but he'd match you. He ketched a frog one day, and took him home, and said he cal'lated to educate him; and so

The Jumping Frog

he never done nothing for three
months but set in his back yard and
learn that frog to jump. And you
bet you he *did* learn him, too. He'd
give him a little punch behind, and
the next minute you'd see that frog
whirling in the air like a doughnut—
see him turn one summerset, or maybe a couple, if he got a good start,
and come down flat-footed and all
right, like a cat. He got him up so
in the matter of ketching flies, and
kep' him in practice so constant, that
he'd nail a fly every time as fur as he
could see him. Smiley said all a frog
wanted was education, and he could
do 'most anything—and I believe him.
Why, I've seen him set Dan'l Webster
down here on this floor—Dan'l Webster was the name of the frog—and

The Jumping Frog

sing out, 'Flies, Dan'l, flies!' and
quicker'n you could wink he'd spring
straight up and snake a fly off'n the
counter there, and flop down on the
floor ag'in as solid as a gob of mud,
and fall to scratching the side of his
head with his hind foot as indifferent
as if he hadn't no idea he'd been
doin' any more'n any frog might do.
You never see a frog so modest and
straightfor'ard as he was, for all he
was so gifted.   And when it come to
fair and square jumping on a dead
level, he could get over more ground
at one straddle than any animal of
his breed you ever see.   Jumping on
a dead level was his strong suit, you
understand; and when it come to that,
Smiley would ante up money on him
as long as he had a red.   Smiley was

17

The Jumping Frog

monstrous proud of his frog, and well he might be, for fellers that had travelled and been everywheres all said he laid over any frog that ever *they* see.

"Well, Smiley kep' the beast in a little lattice box, and he used to fetch him down town sometimes and lay for a bet. One day a feller—a stranger in the camp, he was—come acrost him with his box, and says:

"'What might it be that you've got in the box?'

"And Smiley says, sorter indifferent-like: 'It might be a parrot, or it might be a canary, maybe, but it ain't—it's only just a frog.'

"And the feller took it, and looked at it careful, and turned it round this way and that, and says: 'H'm — so 'tis. Well, what's *he* good for?'

18

"ANDREW JACKSON"

The Jumping Frog

"'Well,' Smiley says, easy and careless, 'he's good enough for *one* thing, I should judge—he can out-jump any frog in Calaveras county.'

" The feller took the box again, and took another long, particular look, and give it back to Smiley, and says, very deliberate, 'Well,' he says, 'I don't see no p'ints about that frog that's any better'n any other frog.'

"'Maybe you don't,' Smiley says. 'Maybe you understand frogs and maybe you don't understand 'em; maybe you've had experience, and maybe you ain't only a amature, as it were. Anyways, I've got *my* opinion, and I'll resk forty dollars that he can outjump any frog in Calaveras county.'

" And the feller studied a minute,

19

and then says, kinder sad like, 'Well, I'm only a stranger here, and I 'ain't got no frog; but if I had a frog, I'd bet you.'

"And then Smiley says, 'That's all right—that's all right—if you'll hold my box a minute, I'll go and get you a frog.' And so the feller took the box, and put up his forty dollars along with Smiley's, and set down to wait.

"So he set there a good while thinking and thinking to hisself, and then he got the frog out and prized his mouth open and took a teaspoon and filled him full of quail shot—filled him pretty near up to his chin—and set him on the floor. Smiley he went to the swamp and slopped around in the mud for a long time, and finally he

The Jumping Frog

ketched a frog, and fetched him in,
and give him to this feller, and says:

"'Now, if you're ready, set him
alongside of Dan'l, with his forepaws
just even with Dan'l's, and I'll give
the word.' Then he says, 'One —
two—three—*git!*' and him and the
feller touched up the frogs from behind, and the new frog hopped off
lively, but Dan'l give a heave, and
hysted up his shoulders—so—like a
Frenchman, but it warn't no use—
he couldn't budge; he was planted as
solid as a church, and he couldn't no
more stir than if he was anchored
out. Smiley was a good deal surprised, and he was disgusted too, but
he didn't have no idea what the matter was, of course.

"The feller took the money and

The Jumping Frog

started away; and when he was going out at the door, he sorter jerked his thumb over his shoulder — so — at Dan'l, and says again, very deliberate, 'Well,' he says, '*I* don't see no p'ints about that frog that's any better'n any other frog.'

"Smiley he stood scratching his head and looking down at Dan'l a long time, and at last he says, 'I do wonder what in the nation that frog throw'd off for — I wonder if there ain't something the matter with him —he 'pears to look mighty baggy, somehow.' And he ketched Dan'l by the nap of the neck, and hefted him, and says, 'Why, blame my cats if he don't weigh five pound!' and turned him upside down and he belched out a double handful of shot.

The Jumping Frog

And then he see how it was, and he was the maddest man—he set the frog down and took out after that feller, but he never ketched him. And—"

[Here Simon Wheeler heard his name called from the front yard, and got up to see what was wanted.] And turning to me as he moved away, he said: "Just set where you are, stranger, and rest easy—I ain't going to be gone a second."

But, by your leave, I did not think that a continuation of the history of the enterprising vagabond *Jim* Smiley would be likely to afford me much information concerning the Rev. *Leonidas W.* Smiley, and so I started away.

At the door I met the sociable Wheeler returning, and he button-holed me and re-commenced:

The Jumping Frog

"Well, thish-yer Smiley had a yaller one-eyed cow that didn't have no tail, only just a short stump like a bannanner, and—"

However, lacking both time and inclination, I did not wait to hear about the afflicted cow, but took my leave.

Now let the learned look upon this picture and say if iconoclasm can further go:

[From the "Revue des Deux Mondes," of July 15, 1872.]

LA GRENOUILLE SANTEUSE DU COMTE DE CALAVERAS

"—Il y avait une fois ici un individu connu sous le nom de Jim Smiley: c'était dans l'hiver de 49, peut-

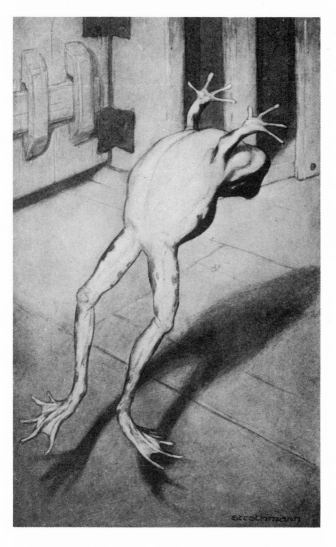

" ' TURN ONE SUMMERSET, OR MAYBE A COUPLE ' "

The Jumping Frog

être bien au printemps de 50, je ne me rappelle pas exactement. Ce qui me fait croire que c'était l'un ou l'autre, c'est que je me souviens que le grand bief n'était pas achevé lorsqu'il arriva au camp pour la premiére fois, mais de toutes façons il était l'homme le plus friand de paris qui se pût voir, pariant sur tout ce qui se présentait, quand il pouvait trouver un adversaire, et, quand il n'en trouvait pas il passait du côté opposé. Tout ce qui convenait à l'autre lui convenait; pourvu qu'il eût un pari, Smiley était satisfait. Et il avait une chance! une chance inouie: presque toujours il gagnait. Il faut dire qu'il était toujours prêt à s'exposer, qu'on ne pouvait mentionner la moindre chose sans que ce gaillard offrît de parier

là-dessus n'importe quoi et de prendre
le côté que l'on voudrait, comme je
vous le disais tout à l'heure. S'il y
avait des courses, vous le trouviez
riche ou ruiné â la fin ; s'il y avait un
combat de chiens, il apportait son
enjeu ; il l'apportait pour un combat
de chats, pour un combat de coqs ;—
parbleu ! si vous aviez vu deux oiseaux
sur une haie, il vous aurait offert de
parier lequel s'envolerait le premier,
et, s'il y avait *meeting* au camp, il
venait parier régulièrement pour le
curé Walker, qu'il jugeait être le
meilleur prédicateur des environs, et
qui l'était en effet, et un brave
homme. Il aurait rencontré une
punaise de bois en chemin, qu'il aurait
parié sur le temps qu'il lui faudrait
pour aller où elle voudrait aller, et, si

The Jumping Frog

vous l'aviez pris au mot, il aurait suivi la punaise jusqu'au Mexique, sans se soucier d'aller si loin, ni du temps qu'il y perdrait. Une fois la femme du curé Walker fut très malade pendant longtemps, il semblait qu'on ne la sauverait pas; mais un matin le curé arrive, et Smiley lui demande comment ella va, et il dit qu'elle est bien mieux, grâce à l'infinie miséricorde, tellement mieux qu'avec la bénédiction de la Providence elle s'en tirerait, et voilá que, sans y penser, Smiley répond : — Eh bien! ye gage deux et demi qu'elle mourra tout de même.

"Ce Smiley avait une jument que les gars appelaient le bidet du quart d'heure, mais seulement pour plaisanter, vous comprenez, parce que,

The Jumping Frog

bien entendu, elle était plus *vite* que
ça! Et il avait coutume de gagner
de l'argent avec cette bête, quoi-
qu'elle fût poussive, cornarde, toujours
prise d'asthme, de coliques ou de con-
somption, ou de quelque chose d'ap-
prochant. On lui donnait 2 ou 300
yards au départ, puis on la dépassait
sans peine ; mais jamais à la fin elle ne
manquait de s'échauffer, de s'exas-
pérer, et elle arrivait, s'écartant, se
défendant, ses jambes grêles en l'air
devant les obstacles, quelquefois les
évitant et faisant avec cela plus de
poussière qu'aucun cheval, plus de
bruit surtout avec ses éternumens et
reniflemens,—crac! elle arrivait donc
toujours première d'une tête, aussi
juste qu'on peut le mesurer. Et
il avait un petit bouledogue qui, à

The Jumping Frog

le voir, ne valait pas un sou; on aurait cru que parier contre lui c'était
voler, tant il était ordinaire; mais
aussitôt les enjeux faits, il devenait
un autre chien. Sa mâchoire inféri-
eure commençait à ressortir comme
un gaillard d'avant, ses dents se
découvraient brillantes commes des
fournaises, et un chien pouvait le
taquiner, l'exciter, le mordre, le jeter
deux ou trois fois par-dessus son
épaule, André Jackson, c'était le nom
du chien, André Jackson prenait cela
tranquillement, comme s'il ne se fût
jamais attendu à autre chose, et
quand les paris étaient doublés et
redoublés contre lui, il vous saisissait
l'autre chien juste à l'articulation de
la jambe de derrière, et il ne la
lâchait plus, non pas qu'il la mâchât,

vous concevez, mais il s'y serait tenu
pendu jusqu'à ce qu'on jetât l'éponge
en l'air, fallût-il attendre un an.
Smiley gagnait toujours avec cette
bête-là; malheureusement ils ont fini
par dresser un chien qui n'avait pas
de pattes de derrière, parce qu'on les
avait sciées, et quand les choses furent
au point qu'il voulait, et qu'il en vint
à se jeter sur son morceau favori, le
pauvre chien comprit en un instant
qu'on s'était moqué de lui, et que
l'autre le tenait. Vous n'avez jamais
vu personne avoir l'air plus penaud
et plus découragé; il ne fit aucun
effort pour gagner le combat et fut
rudement secoué, de sorte que, re-
gardant Smiley comme pour lui dire:
—Mon cœur est brisé, c'est ta faute;
pourquoi m'avoir livré à un chien qui

"DAN'L WEBSTER"

The Jumping Frog

n'a pas de pattes de derriére, puisque
c'est par là que je les bats?—il s'en
alla en clopinant, et se coucha pour
mourir. Ah! c'était un bon chien,
cet André Jackson, et il se serait fait
un nom, s'il avait vécu, car il y avait
de l'etoffe en lui, il avait du génie,
je la sais, bien que de grandes occa-
sions lui aient manqué; mais il est
impossible de supposer qu'un chien
capable de se battre comme lui, cer-
taines circonstances étant donées, ait
manqué de talent. Je me sens triste
toutes les fois que je pense à son
dernier combat et au dénoûment
qu'il a eu. Eh bien! ce Smiley nour-
rissait des terriers à rats, et des coqs
de combat, et des chats, et toute sorte
de choses, au point qu'il était toujours en mesure de vous tenir tête, et

The Jumping Frog

qu'avec sa rage de paris on n'avait
plus de repos. Il attrapa un jour une
grenouille et l'emporta chez lui, disant
qu'il prétendait faire son éducation;
vous me croirez si vous voulez, mais
pendant trois mois il n'a rien fait que
lui apprendre à sauter dans une cour
retirée de sa maison. Et je vous
réponds qu'il avait réussi. Il lui
donnait un petit coup par derrière, et
l'instant d'après vous voyiez la grenouille tourner en l'air comme un
beignet au-dessus de la poêle, faire
une culbute, quelquefois deux, lorsqu'elle était bien partie, et retomber
sur ses pattes comme un chat. Il
l'avait dressée dans l'art de gober des
mouches, et l'y exerçait continuelle-
ment, si bien qu'une mouche, du plus
loin qu'elle apparaissait, était une

The Jumping Frog

mouche perdue. Smiley avait coutume de dire que tout ce qui manquait à une grenouille, c'était l'éducation, qu'avec l'éducation elle pouvait faire presque tout, et je le crois. Tenez, je l'ai vu poser Daniel Webster là sur se plancher, — Daniel Webster était le nom de la grenouille, — et lui chanter:—Des mouches! Daniel, des mouches!—En un clin d'œil, Daniel avait bondi et saisi une mouche ici sur le comptoir, puis sauté de nouveau par terre, où il restait vraiment à se gratter la tête avec sa patte de derrière, comme s'il n'avait pas eu la moindre idée de sa supériorité. Jamais vous n'avez grenouille vu de aussi modeste, aussi naturelle, douée comme elle l'était! Et quand il s'agissait de sauter purement et simplement

sur terrain plat, elle faisait plus de
chemin en un saut qu'aucune bête de
son espèce que vous puissiez connaître.
Sauter à plat, c'était son fort! Quand
il s'agaissait de cela, Smiley entassait
les enjeux sur elle tant qu'il lui, restait
un rouge liard.   Il faut le reconnaître,
Smiley était monstrueusement fier de
sa grenouille, et il en avait le droit,
car des gens qui avaient voyagé, qui
avaient tout vu, disaient qu'on lui
ferait injure de la comparer à une
autre; de façon que Smiley gardait
Daniel dans une petite boîte à claire-
voie qu'il emporta it parfois à la ville
pour quelque pari.

"Un jour, un individu étranger au
camp l'arrête avec sa boîte et lui dit:
—Qu'est-ce que vous avez donc serré
là dedans?

The Jumping Frog

"Smiley dit d'un air indifférent:—
Cela pourrait être un perroquet ou
un serin, mais ce n'est rien de pareil,
ce n'est qu'une grenouille.

"L'individu la prend, la regarde
avec soin, la tourne d'un côté et de
l'autre, puss il dit.—Tiens! en effet!
A quoi est-elle bonne?

"—Mon Dieu! répond Smiley, toujours d'un air dégagé, elle est bonne
pour une chose à mon avis, elle peut
battre en sautant toute grenouille du
comté de Calaveras.

"L'individu reprend la boîte, l'examine de nouveau longuement, et la
rend à Smiley en disant d'un air délibéré:—Eh bien! je ne vois pas que
cette grenouille ait rien de mieux
qu'aucune grenouille.

"—Possible que vous ne le voyiez

paz, dit Smiley, possible que vous
vous entendiez en grenouilles, possible que vous ne vous y entendez
point, possible que vous ayez de l'ex-
périence, et possible que vous ne soyez
qu'un amateur. De toute manière, je
parie quarante dollars qu'elle battra
en sautant n'importe quelle grenouille
du comté de Calaveras.

"L'individu réfléchit une seconde
et dit comme attristé:—Je ne suis
qu'un étranger ici, je n'ai pas de
grenouille; mais, si j'en avais une, je
tiendrais le pari.

"—Fort bien! répond Smiley.
Rien de plus facile. Si vous voulez
tenir ma boîte une minute, j'irai vous
chercher une grenouille.—Voilà donc
l'individu qui garde la boîte, qui met
ses quarante dollars sur ceux de

"'IT MIGHT BE A CANARY, MAYBE, BUT IT AIN'T—IT'S ONLY
JUST A FROG'"

The Jumping Frog

Smiley et qui attend. Il attend assez longtemps, réfléchissant tout seul, et figurez - vous qu'il prend Daniel, lui ouvre la bouche de force et avec une cuiller à thé l'emplit de menu plomb de chasse, mais l'emplit jusqu'au menton, puis il le pose par terre. Smiley pendant ce temps était à barboter dans une mare. Finalement il attrape une grenouille, l'apporte à cet individu et dit:—Maintenant, si vous êtes prêt, mettez-la tout contre Daniel, avec leurs pattes de devant sur la même ligne, et je donnerai le signal;—puis il ajoute:—Un, deux, trois, sautez!

"Lui et l'individu touchent leurs grenouilles par derrière, et la grenouille neuve se met à sautiller, mais Daniel se soulève lourdement, hausse

The Jumping Frog

les épaules ainsi, comme un Français;
à quoi bon? il ne pouvait bouger, il
était planté solide comme une en-
clume, il n'avançait pas puls que si
on l'eût mis á l'ancre. Smiley fut
surpris et dégoûté, mais il ne se
doutait pas du tour, bien entendu.
L'individu empoche l'argent, s'en va,
et en s'en allant est-ce qu'il ne donne
pas un coup de pouce par-dessus
lé'paule, comme ça, au pauvre Daniel, en disant de son air délibéré:—
Eh bien! je ne vois pas que cette
grenouille ait rien de mieux qu'une
autre.

"Smiley se gratta longtemps la
tête, les yeux fixés sur Daniel, jusqu'à ce qu'enfin il dit:—Je me demande comment diable il se fait que
cette bête ait refusé. . . . Est-ce

The Jumping Frog

qu'elle aurait quelque chose? . . . On croirait qu'elle est enflée.

"Il empoigne Daniel par la peau du cou, le souléve et dit:—Le loup me croque, s'il ne pèse pas cinq livres.

"Il le retourne, et le malheureux crache deux poignées de plomb. Quand Smiley reconnut ce qui en était, il fut comme fou. Vous le voyez d'ici poser sa grenouille par terre et courir aprés cet individu, mais il ne le rattrapa jamais, et" . . .

[Translation of the above back from the French.]

THE FROG JUMPING OF THE COUNTY
OF CALAVERAS

It there was one time here an individual known under the name of Jim Smiley; it was in the winter of

The Jumping Frog

'49, possibly well at the spring of '50,
I no me recollect not exactly. This
which me makes to believe that it
was the one or the other, it is that I
shall remember that the grand flume
is not achieved when he arrives at
the camp for the first time, but of all
sides he was the man the most fond
of to bet which one have seen, betting upon all that which is presented,
when he could find an adversary; and
when he not of it could not, he passed
to the side opposed. All that which
convenienced to the other, to him
convenienced also; seeing that he had
a bet, Smiley was satisfied. And he
had a chance! a chance even worth-
less; nearly always he gained. It
must to say that he was always near
to himself expose, but one no could

The Jumping Frog

mention the least thing without that
this gaillard offered to bet the bot-
tom, no matter what, and to take
the side that one him would, as I
you it said all at the hour (tout à
l'heure). If it there was of races,
you him find rich or ruined at the
end; if it there is a combat of dogs,
he bring his bet; he himself laid always for a combat of cats, for a combat of cocks;—by-blue! If you have
see two birds upon a fence, he you
should have offered of to bet which
of those birds shall fly the first; and
if there is *meeting* at the camp (*meeting* au camp) he comes to bet regu-
larly for the curé Walker, which he
judged to be the best predicator of
the neighborhood (prédicateur des
environs) and which he was in effect,

The Jumping Frog

and a brave man. He would en-
counter a bug of wood in the road,
whom he will bet upon the time
which he shall take to go where she
would go—and if you him have take
at the word, he will follow the bug
as far as Mexique, without himself
caring to go so far; neither of the
time which he there lost. One time
the woman of the curé Walker is very
sick during long time, it seemed that
one not her saved not; but one morning the curé arrives, and Smiley him
demanded how she goes, and he said
that she is well better, grace to the
infinite misery (lui demande comment elle va, et il dit qu'elle est bien
mieux, grâce à l'infinie misèricorde),
so much better that with the bene-
diction of the Providence she herself

"'PRIZED HIS MOUTH OPEN'"

of it would pull out (elle s'en tirerait);
and behold that without there thinking Smiley responds: "Well, I gage
two-and-half that she will die all of
same."

This Smiley had an animal which
the boys called the nag of the quarter
of hour, but solely for pleasantry,
you comprehend, because, well understand, she was more fast as that!
[Now, why that exclamation?—M. T.]
And it was custom of to gain of the
silver with this beast, notwithstand-
ing she was poussive, cornarde, always taken of asthma, of colics, or of
consumption, or something of ap-
proaching. One him would give two
or three hundred yards at the depart-
ure, then one him passed without
pain; but never at the last she not

43

fail of herself èchauffer, of herself
exasperate, and she arrives herself
écartant, se dèfendant, her legs grêles
in the air before the obstacles, sometimes them elevating and making with
this more of dust than any horse,
more of noise above with his éternumens and reniflemens—crac! she arrives then always first by one head, as
just as one can it measure. And he
had a small bull dog (boule dogue!)
who, to him see, no value, not a cent;
one would believe that to bet against
him it was to steal, so much he was
ordinary; but as soon as the game
made, she becomes another dog. Her
jaw inferior commence to project like
a deck of before, his teeth themselves
discover brilliant like some furnaces,
and a dog could him tackle (le

The Jumping Frog

taquiner), him excite, him murder (le
mordre), him throw two or three
times over his shoulder, André Jackson—this was the name of the dog—
André Jackson takes that tranquilly,
as if he not himself was never ex-
pecting other thing, and when the
bets were doubled and redoubled
against him, he you seize the other
dog just at the articulation of the leg
of behind, and he not it leave more,
not that he it masticate, you conceive,
but he himself there shall be hold-
ing during until that one throws the
sponge in the air, must he wait a year.
Smiley gained always with this beast-
là; unhappily they have finished by
elevating a dog who no had not of
feet of behind, because one them had
sawed; and when things were at the

45

The Jumping Frog

point that he would, and that he
came to himself throw upon his
morsel favorite, the poor dog com-
prehended in an instant that he himself was deceived in him, and that the
other dog him had. You no have
never see person having the air more
penaud and more discouraged; he not
made no effort to gain the combat,
and was rudely shucked.

Eh bien! this Smiley nourished
some terriers à rats, and some cocks
of combat, and some cats, and all
sorts of things; and with his rage of
betting one no had more of repose.
He trapped one day a frog and him
imported with him (et l'emporta chez
lui), saying that he pretended to make
his education.   You me believe if you
will, but during three months he not

The Jumping Frog

has nothing done but to him appre-
hend to jump (apprendre ă sauter)
in a court retired of her mansion (de
sa maison). And I you respond that
he have succeeded. He him gives a
small blow by behind, and the instant
after you shall see the frog turn in the
air like a grease-biscuit, make one sum-
mersault, sometimes two, when she
was well started, and re-fall upon his
feet like a cat. He him had accom-
plished in the art of to gobble the
flies (gober des mouches), and him
there exercised continually—so well
that a fly at the most far that she
appeared was a fly lost. Smiley had
custom to say that all which lacked
to a frog it was the education, but
with the education she could do nearly
all — and I him believe.   Tenez, I

The Jumping Frog

him have seen pose Daniel Webster there upon this plank—Daniel Webster was the name of the frog—and to him sing, "Some flies, Daniel, some flies!"—in a flash of the eye Daniel had bounded and seized a fly here upon the counter, then jumped anew at the earth, where he rested truly to himself scratch the head with his behind foot, as if he no had not the least idea of his superiority. Never you not have seen frog as modest, as natural, sweet as she was. And when he himself agitated to jump purely and simply upon plain earth, she does more ground in one jump than any beast of his species than you can know. To jump plain —this was his strong. When he himself agitated for that, Smiley multi-

48

"'FINALLY HE KETCHED A FROG'"

The Jumping Frog

plied the bets upon her as long as there to him remained a red. It must to know, Smiley was monstrously proud of his frog, and he of it was right, for some men who were traveled, who had all seen, said that they to him would be injurious to him compare to another frog. Smiley guarded Daniel in a little box latticed which he carried bytimes to the village for some bet.

One day an individual stranger at the camp him arrested with his box and him said:

"What is this that you have then shut up there within?"

Smiley said, with an air indifferent:

"That could be a paroquet, or a syringe (ou un serin), but this no is nothing of such, it not is but a frog."

49

The Jumping Frog

The individual it took, it regarded with care, it turned from one side and from the other, then he said:

"Tiens! in effect!—At what is she good?"

"My God!" respond Smiley, always with an air disengaged, "she is good for one thing, to my notice (à mon avis), she can batter in jumping (elle peut batter en sautant) all frogs of the county of Calaveras."

The individual re-took the box, it examined of new longly, and it rendered to Smiley in saying with an air deliberate:

"Eh bien! I no saw not that that frog had nothing of better than each frog." (Je ne vois pas que cette grenouille ait rien de mieux qu'aucune grenouille.) [If that isn't grammar gone to seed, then I count myself no judge.—M. T.]

"Possible that you not it saw not," said Smiley, "possible that you—you comprehend frogs; possible that you not you there comprehend nothing; possible that you had of the experience, and possible that you not be but an amateur. Of all manner (De toute manière) I bet forty dollars that she batter in jumping no matter which frog of the county of Calaveras."

The individual reflected a second, and said like sad:

"I not am but a stranger here, I no have not a frog; but if I of it had one, I would embrace the bet."

"Strong well!" respond Smiley; "nothing of more facility. If you

The Jumping Frog

will hold my box a minute, I go you to search a frog (j'irai vous chercher)."

Behold, then, the individual, who guards the box, who puts his forty dollars upon those of Smiley, and who attends (et qui attend). He attended enough longtimes, reflecting all solely. And figure you that he takes Daniel, him opens the mouth by force and with a teaspoon him fills with shot of the hunt, even him fills just to the chin, then he him puts by the earth. Smiley during these times was at slopping in a swamp. Finally he trapped (attrape) a frog, him carried to that individual, and said:

"Now if you be ready, put him all against Daniel, with their before feet upon the same line, and I give the

"'TURNED HIM UPSIDE DOWN'"

The Jumping Frog

signal"—then he added: "One, two, three—advance!"

Him and the individual touched their frogs by behind, and the frog new put to jump smartly, but Daniel himself lifted ponderously, exalted the shoulders thus, like a Frenchman—to what good? he not could budge, he is planted solid like a church, he not advance no more than if one him had put at the anchor.

Smiley was surprised and disgusted, but he not himself doubted not of the turn being intended (mais il ne se doutait pas du tour, bien entendu). The individual empocketed the silver, himself with it went, and of it himself in going is it that he no gives not a jerk of thumb over the shoulder—like that—at the poor Daniel, in say-

The Jumping Frog

ing with his air deliberate—(L'individu empoche l'argent, s'en va et en s'en allant est ce qu'il ne donne pas un coup de pouce par-dessus l'épaule, comme ca, au pauvre Daniel, endisant de son air délibéré):

"Eh bien! *I no see not that that frog has nothing of better than another.*"

Smiley himself scratched longtimes the head, the eyes fixed upon Daniel, until that which at last he said:

"I me demand how the devil it makes itself that this beast has refused. Is it that she had something? One would believe that she is stuffed."

He grasped Daniel by the skin of the neck, him lifted and said:

"The wolf me bite if he no weigh not five pounds."

The Jumping Frog

He him reversed and the unhappy belched two handfuls of shot (et le malhereus, etc.). When Smiley recognized how it was, he was like mad. He deposited his frog by the earth and ran after that individual, but he not him caught never.

Such is the Jumping Frog, to the distorted French eye. I claim that I never put together such an odious mixture of bad grammar and delirium tremens in my life. And what has a poor foreigner like me done, to be abused and misrepresented like this? When I say, "Well, I don't see no p'ints about that frog that's any better'n any other frog," is it kind, is it just, for this Frenchman to try to make it appear that I said, "Eh bien!

The Jumping Frog

I no saw not that that frog had nothing of better than each frog?" I have no heart to write more. I never felt so about anything before.

HARTFORD, March, 1875.

PRIVATE HISTORY OF THE "JUMPING FROG" STORY

Five or six years ago a lady from Finland asked me to tell her a story in our negro dialect, so that she could get an idea of what that variety of speech was like. I told her one of Hopkinson Smith's negro stories, and gave her a copy of *Harper's Monthly* containing it. She translated it for a Swedish newspaper, but by an oversight named me as the author of it instead of

56

"MY RE-TRANSLATION FROM THE FRENCH"

The Jumping Frog

Smith. I was very sorry for that, because I got a good lashing in the Swedish press, which would have fallen to his share but for that mistake; for it was shown that Boccaccio had told that very story, in his curt and meagre fashion, five hundred years before Smith took hold of it and made a good and tellable thing out of it.

I have always been sorry for Smith. But my own turn has come now. A few weeks ago Professor Van Dyke, of Princeton, asked this question:

"Do you know how old your Jumping Frog story is?"

And I answered:

"Yes—forty-five years. The thing happened in Calaveras County in the spring of 1849."

The Jumping Frog

"No; it happened earlier—a couple of thousand years earlier; it is a Greek story."

I was astonished—and hurt. I said:

"I am willing to be a literary thief if it has been so ordained; I am even willing to be caught robbing the ancient dead alongside of Hopkinson Smith, for he is my friend and a good fellow, and I think would be as honest as any one if he could do it without occasioning remark; but I am not willing to antedate his crimes by fifteen hundred years. I must ask you to knock off part of that."

But the professor was not chaffing; he was in earnest, and could not abate a century. He named the Greek author, and offered to get the

The Jumping Frog

book and send it to me and the col-
lege text-book containing the English
translation also. I thought I would
like the translation best, because
Greek makes me tired. January 30th
he sent me the English version, and
I will presently insert it in this
article. It is my Jumping Frog tale
in every essential. It is not strung
out as I have it strung out, but it is
all there.

To me this is very curious and interesting. Curious for several rea-
sons. For instance:

I heard the story told by a man
who was not telling it to his hearers
as a thing new to them, but as a
thing which *they had witnessed and
would remember*. He was a dull person, and ignorant; he had no gift as

The Jumping Frog

a story-teller, and no invention; in
his mouth this episode was merely
history—history and statistics; and
the gravest sort of history, too; he
was entirely serious, for he was deal-
ing with what to him were austere
facts, and they interested him solely
because they *were* facts; he was draw-
ing on his memory, not his mind; he
saw no humor in his tale, neither did
his listeners; neither he nor they ever
smiled or laughed; in my time I have
not attended a more solemn confer-
ence.   To him and to his fellow gold-
miners there were just two things in
the story that were worth considering.
One was the smartness of its hero, Jim
Smiley,* in taking the stranger in with
a loaded frog; and the other was
Smiley's deep knowledge of a frog's

*[Editor's Note: Mark Twain appears to
have confused the two characters at this
point.]

The Jumping Frog

nature—for he knew (as the narrator asserted and the listeners conceded) that a frog *likes shot* and is always ready to eat it. Those men discussed those two points, and those only. They were hearty in their admiration of them, and none of the party was aware that a first-rate story had been told in a first-rate way, and that it was brimful of a quality whose presence they never suspected—humor.

Now, then, the interesting question is, *did* the frog episode happen in Angel's Camp in the spring of '49, as told in my hearing that day in the fall of 1865? I am perfectly sure that it did. I am also sure that its duplicate happened in Bœotia a couple of thousand years ago. I think it must be a case of history

The Jumping Frog

actually repeating itself, and not a case of a good story floating down the ages and surviving because too good to be allowed to perish.

I would now like to have the reader examine the Greek story and the story told by the dull and solemn Californian, and observe how exactly alike they are in essentials.

[*Translation.*]

THE ATHENIAN AND THE FROG*

An Athenian once fell in with a Bœotian who was sitting by the road-side looking at a frog. Seeing the other approach, the Bœotian said his was a remarkable frog, and asked if he would agree to start a contest of

* Sidgwick, *Greek Prose Composition*, p. 116.

The Jumping Frog

frogs, on condition that he whose frog jumped farthest should receive a large sum of money. The Athenian replied that he would if the other would fetch him a frog, for the lake was near. To this he agreed, and when he was gone the Athenian took the frog, and, opening its mouth, poured some stones into its stomach, so that it did not indeed seem larger than before, but could not jump. The Bœotian soon returned with the other frog, and the contest began. The second frog first was pinched, and jumped moderately; then they pinched the Bœotian frog. And he gathered himself for a leap, and used the utmost effort, but he could not move his body the least. So the Athenian departed with the money.

The Jumping Frog

When he was gone the Bœotian, wondering what was the matter with the frog, lifted him up and examined him. And being turned upside down, he opened his mouth and vomited out the stones.

NOTE. *November*, 1903. When I became convinced that the "Jumping Frog" was a Greek story two or three thousand years old, I was sincerely happy, for apparently here was a most striking and satisfactory justification of a favorite theory of mine —to wit, that no *occurrence* is sole and solitary, but is merely a repetition of a thing which has happened before, and perhaps often. Still, when I later had a chance to see Professor Sidgwick's book I was a little staggered,

The Jumping Frog

because of two things: the details were a little *too* faithful to the facts in the Calaveras incident for the comfort of my theory, and I could not help being suspicious of the Greek frog because he was willing to be fed with gravel. One can't beguile the modern frog with that product.

By-and-by, in England, after a few years, I learned that there hadn't been any Greek frog in the business, and no Greek story about his adventures. Professor Sidgwick had not claimed that it was a Greek tale; he had merely synopsised the Calaveras tale and transferred the incident to classic Greece; but as he did not state that it was the same old frog, the English papers reproved him for the omission. He told me this in England in 1899 or

The Jumping Frog

1900, and was much troubled about that censure, for his act had been innocent, he believing that the story's origin was so well known as to render formal mention of it unnecessary. I was very sorry for the censure, but it was not I that applied it. I would not have done it.

M. T.

THE END